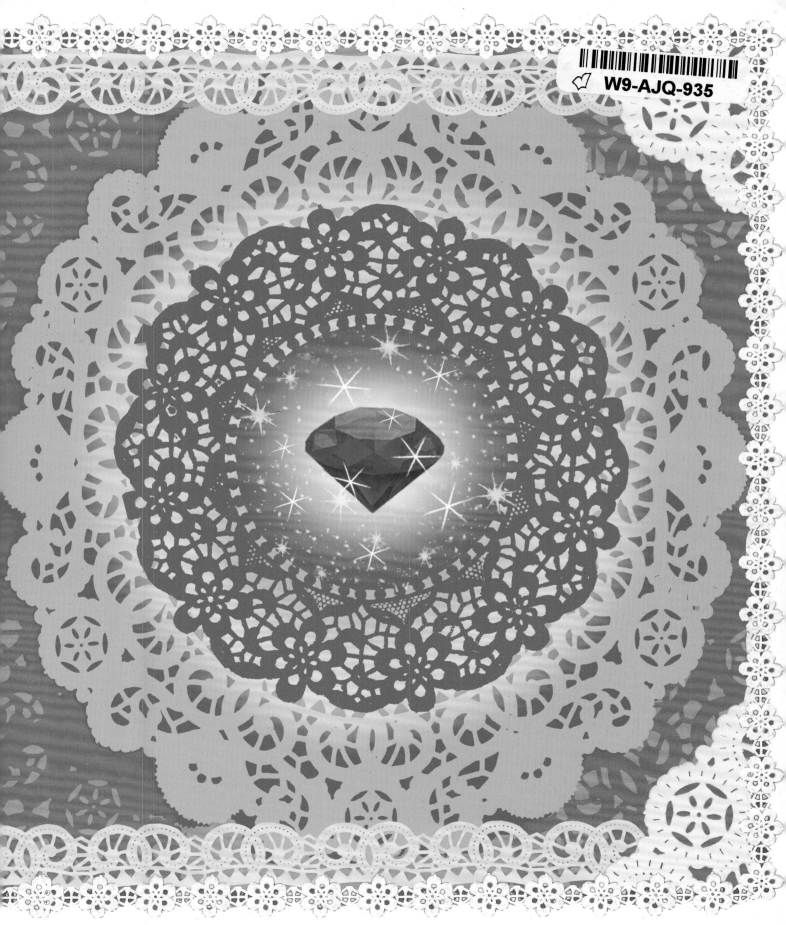

Rubylicious

WRITTEN AND ILLUSTRATED BY
Victoria Kann

HARPER
An Imprint of HarperCollinsPublishers

While playing, I found a little stone for my rock collection.

"I love all my rocks, but I love this one the most because it is my one hundredth rock!" I said, showing my collection to Peter, my brother.

"That rock is old and dirty," said Peter.

"I can clean it," I said, rubbing it with a cloth. "See? It was dirty and now it's . . . ummm . . . ah . . . still dirty."

Peter picked up the cloth and started rubbing the rock.
"I don't know, Pinkalicious. I think you could find a nicer rock
than this one."

Suddenly, the room filled
with a poof of red smoke
and a figure appeared.

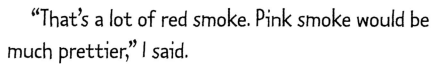

"That's a lot of red smoke. Pink smoke would be much prettier," I said.

"Red is a pretty color too. Just think of it as very dark pink," said the figure. "You found my home on the luckiest of days, when all the rotating hemispheric coordinates are aligned with the number one hundred," said the figure. "So you now have me, your very own granter of wishes. Congratulations!"

"Wishes?! Wow, are you a genie?" asked Peter.

"Aren't genies supposed to be in a bottle?" I asked.

"I am not a genie. I wouldn't live in a bottle because bottles get recycled," she said. "I can live anywhere, in trees or even rocks."

"OK, we'll call you Rocky," I said.

"I guess that's fine for now. You get one wish. After I grant your wish, I am free to go," said Rocky.

"I thought genies gave three wishes,
not one," said Peter.

"As I said, I am not a genie. I grant one wish, no
more. Granting wishes scares me. You never know
how they're going to turn out," Rocky said.

"Can I wish for a pile of sweets?" I asked.

"That sounds like a wonderful wish, but I'm not sure," Rocky said nervously. "Let me show you first—then you can decide."

POOF! A big cloud of smoke swirled around us. Suddenly, we were standing on top of a giant mountain of candy, cupcakes, cookies, and ice cream.

"WOW! This is sweetatastic!" Peter and I shrieked with happiness, trying to eat as much as possible.

"What's wrong, Rocky?" I asked.
"I'm worried about how this wish will turn out. Is this
your very best wish, your most favorite thing in the world?"
she asked us meekly.

"It's pretty amazing," said Peter, "but my stomach hurts. I ate too much."

"And my head aches from so much sugar," I said.
The candy started to melt into a colorful swirl and we began to sink into it.

"Maybe this isn't a very good wish," I said.

"Let's go back to your house and eat something healthy. Can you wish for something else?" Rocky asked.

"What if I wished that we could fly?" asked Peter.

"Oh dear, oh dearie dear, would that be the very best wish? Is that what you want more than anything else in the entire world?" Rocky asked.

"YES!!!!!!!" said Peter.

"Then I will show you your wish," she said, her voice shaking.

POOF! A cloud of smoke formed around us as we floated out the window and into the sky on a flying machine.

"This is fun-errific!" I screamed while we zipped toward the clouds.

"Whooooaaaah! Be . . . be . . . be . . . careful . . . ," Rocky said anxiously.

"Look out for the bird, Pinkalicious!" Peter hollered.

"PETER, watch out for that plane!" I yelled.

"Eeeeeeek!" Rocky screeched.

"This might not be the very best wish. Let's think of something else," I said.

"Yes, please, something safe," begged Rocky.

"I have always wished to be a princess in a castle," I said.

"And I could be a prince!" said Peter.

"OK, if that's your very best, most favorite wish ever," Rocky said doubtfully. POOF! A puff of smoke revealed a beautiful castle.

"Wow, it's pinkamazing!" I said.

"Yes . . . everyone thinks they want a castle." Rocky sighed.

"Where are you, Peter? This castle is so big and cold!" I was shivering.

"I'm by the drawbridge. There's something in the moat," said Peter.

"Careful of the alligator, and watch out for the fire-breathing dragon!" yelled Rocky.

"A . . . a . . . achooooooo!"
Rocky sneezed. "I'm freezing and
frightened."

"Brrrrrr, maybe wishing for a
castle isn't the very best wish.
Let's go home," I said.

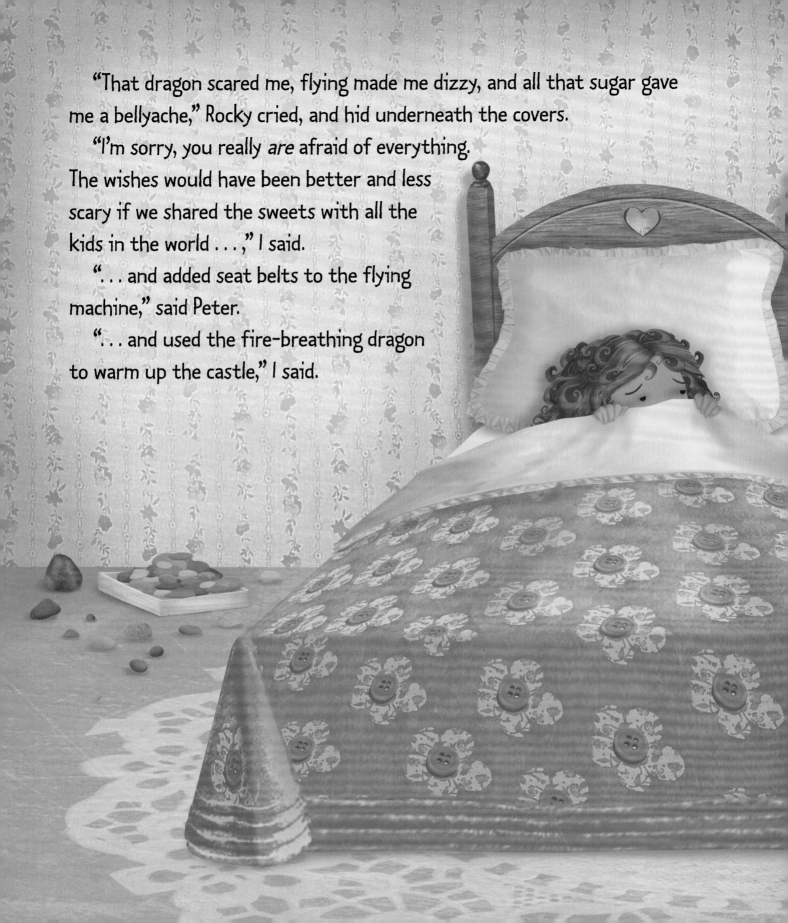

"That dragon scared me, flying made me dizzy, and all that sugar gave me a bellyache," Rocky cried, and hid underneath the covers.

"I'm sorry, you really *are* afraid of everything. The wishes would have been better and less scary if we shared the sweets with all the kids in the world . . . ," I said.

". . . and added seat belts to the flying machine," said Peter.

". . . and used the fire-breathing dragon to warm up the castle," I said.

"I was too scared to think of that," said Rocky.

"I wish you were brave, because then you wouldn't be afraid, and then you would have more fun," I said. "That would be our very best . . ."

"Most favorite . . . ," Peter added.

"Wish in the whole wide world," I said.

"Pinkalicious and Peter, you made a wish for me?!" said Rocky.

Smoke swirled around her and she began to sparkle and shimmer. So did her rock.

I held it in my hand as it glittered. "It's . . . it's . . . it's a ruby!" I said.

"That's right! My real name is Ruby. I have been cursed for a hundred years by someone who didn't like their wish. You broke the curse on this lucky day when you generously made a wish for *me*!" said Ruby.

Ruby swirled around. "I'm not a genie, but I am a genius! Now that I'm not scared, I can grant your wishes."

POOF! "Here is a castle. It's a little smaller, without dragons and alligators. I hope you enjoy your new flying machine. It has seat belts and helmets. It travels slower and doesn't go very high, but you can make it go upside down and sideways."

"Wheeeeeee!" I said, trying it out.

"Lastly, here are nutritious lollipops, guaranteed to last forever," Ruby said.

Peter and I hugged her. "Thank you, Ruby, they are . . . RUBYLICIOUS!" we yelled together.